Archie's Lucky E
Woodlice World

Written by Patrick Caruth
Illustrated by Jenny Noscoe
ISBN 978-0-9570939-0-4

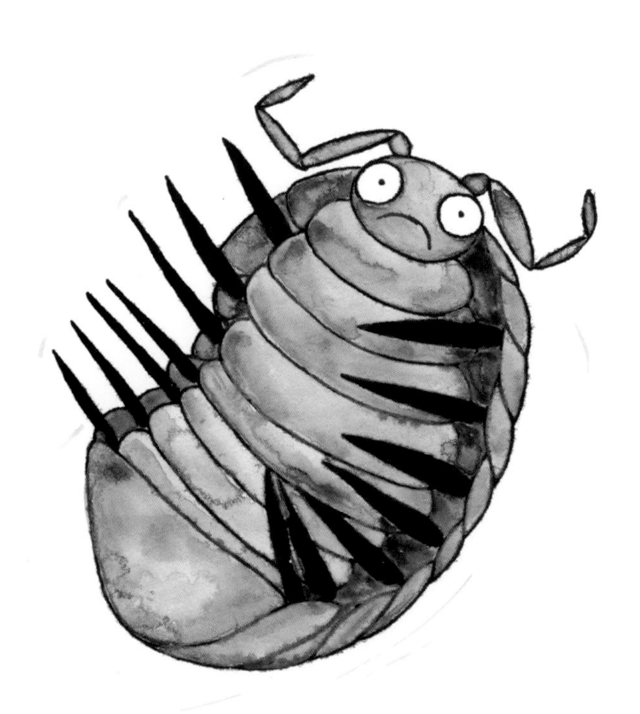

Published by Patrick Caruth

One day Archie and Pam were having lunch with their friend Neville.

Afterwards they decided to go
and play in the vegetable garden.

When they got there they
found a tall clump of rhubarb.

"Lets climb up them!"
said Neville.

Pam was a bit scared,
they were very high.

They started to climb.
This is fun thought Archie.

Soon it got windy and the rhubarb started swaying.

There was a gust of wind and SUDDENLY...

HELP!!

Shouted Archie.

A gust of wind had blown him
off the leaf and he was flying through the air...

...and was heading straight towards a **large** cobweb!

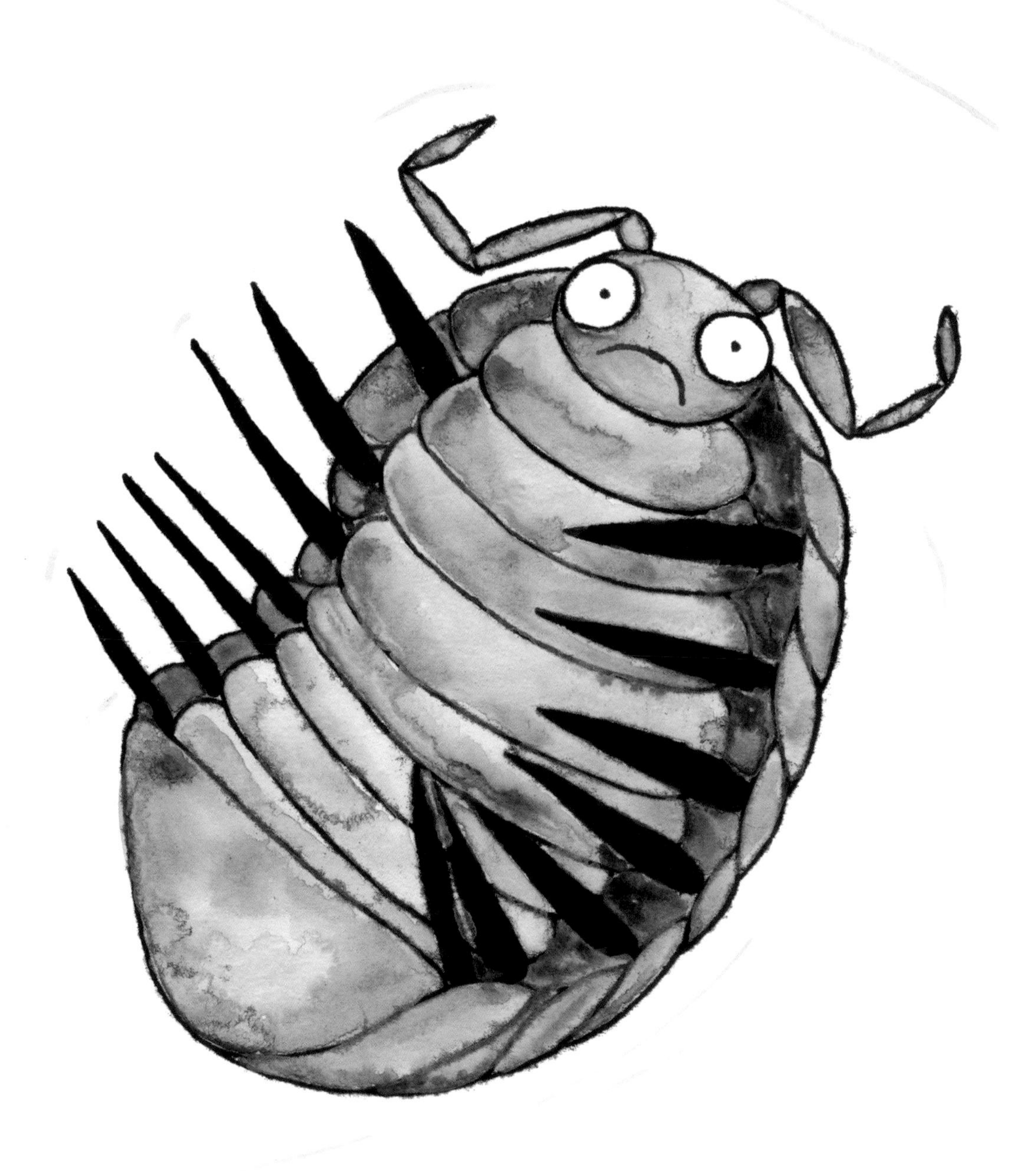

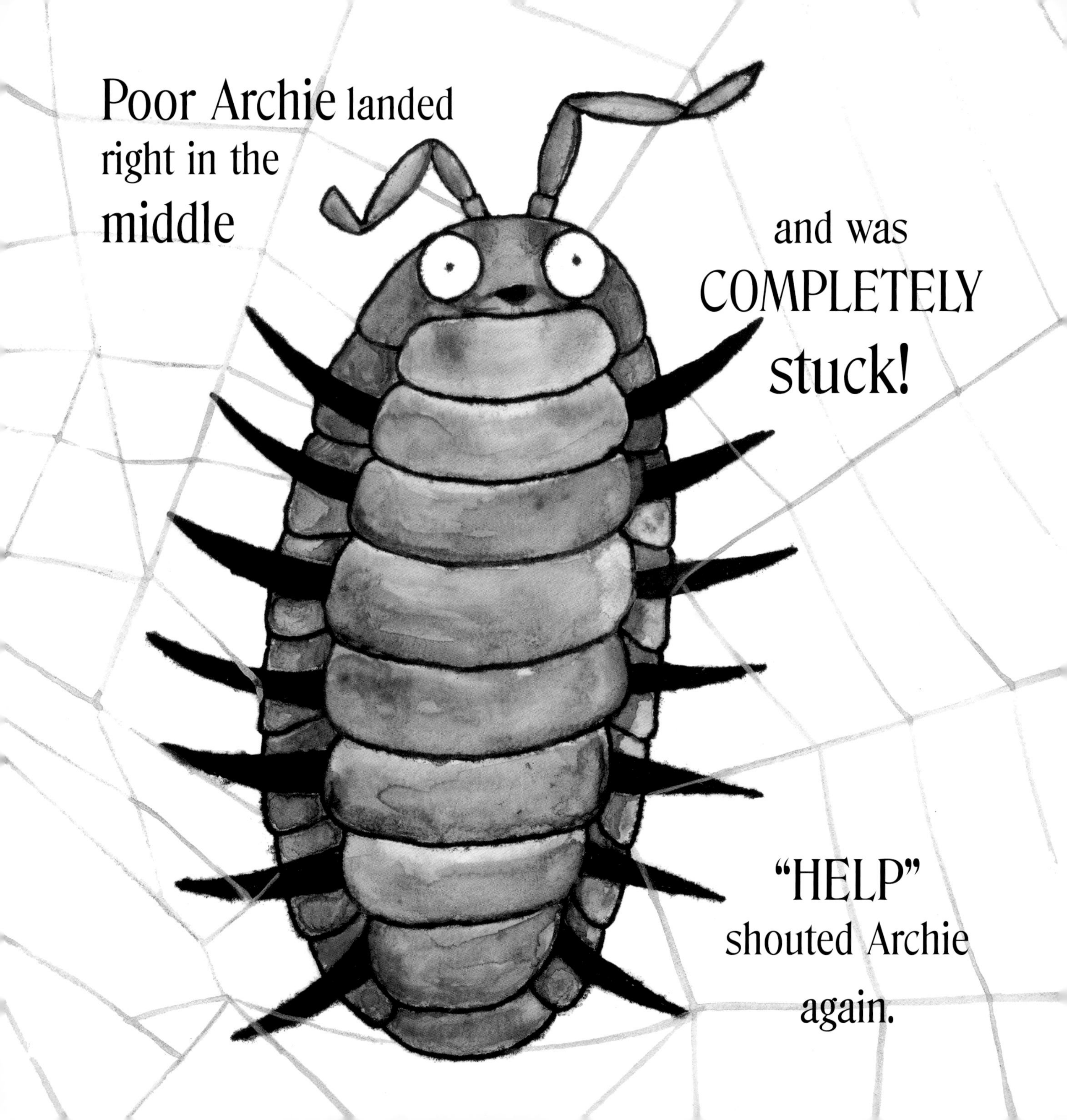
Poor Archie landed
right in the
middle
and was
COMPLETELY
stuck!
"HELP"
shouted Archie
again.

The cobweb belonged to a scary spider called Priscilla.

She was hoping to catch a fat juicy fly and was very cross when she saw a woodlouse.

"You've messed up my cobweb!" she screamed.

"You will have to stay there until I have caught a fly".

The other woodlice had seen what had happened and came running.

"We must rescue him" said Pam.

"But how can we do it?"

"I've got a plan" said Neville, "But we need Beryl's help"

They all huddled round while Neville explained his plan.

Beryl was a friendly blackbird, and they found her on the lawn pulling up worms.
They told her about Archie and how they needed her help.

Neville explained his plan.

Beryl wasn't sure, especially as it involved Maxwell,
the Grumpy Tomcat.
"Maxwell eats blackbirds for breakfast you know"
"OH PLEASE"
shouted all the woodlice.

Beryl thought for a while and then said.

"Alright, I will help"

"Thank you" said Neville.

"Follow us."

And they raced off
to rescue Archie.

In the corner of the garden they
found Maxwell fast asleep.

Archie, meanwhile was feeling very sad and lonely.
The more he wriggled, the more he got stuck.
But help was coming...

... Down the path, Beryl crept towards Maxwell. She took a deep breath and gave a loud SQUAWK.

Maxwell's eyes shot open.

He saw Beryl and quick as a flash...

He raced after Beryl who flapped all the way down the path towards the cobweb...

FASTER and FASTER until Beryl suddenly flew away and...

Too late he realised he would run straight into it...

The cobweb fell onto Maxwell and covered him with gooey strands. He glared angrily, knowing he had been tricked.

But Archie was finally free!

Priscilla shouted angrily
"Look what you have done
to my cobweb!!"
"Thank you Beryl"
cheered the Woodlice, and they
all went home for tea.

Also in the series....

Woodlice world 'The Rolling Race'
Archie and Pam are two very special Woodlice who live at the bottom of the garden under a flowerpot.
The Rolling Race ias a story of their adventures through the garden, meeting lots of friends and very nearly a watery end!

Look out for more adventures and visit Archie and Pam at
www.woodliceworld.com

Patrick Caruth
When Patrick's young children discovered woodlice under the flowerpots he decided to write a story about them and Woodlice World was born.
Patrick is also an airline pilot and lives in Somerset with his family and garden full of woodlice and their friends!

Jenny Noscoe
Jenny grew up in dorset. She studied BA (hons) Illustration at Falmouth College of Arts. She is an illustrator of children's books as well as drawing illustrations for editorial, narrative and advertising copy.
If you are interested and would like to see more of Jenny's work please visit
www.jennynoscoe.co.uk

Published by Patrick Caruth
First Edition published 2011

Printed by Shelleys of Sherborne

ISBN 978-0-9570939-0-4